THIS BOOK
IS FOR:

OLIVE THE FRENCHIE IS READY FOR A BIG DAY, BUT WHAT TO DO? SHE REMEMBERS HER FAVORITE PASTIME - NAPPING!

EVEN THOUGH SHE IS TIRED OLIVE BEGINS HER SEARCH FOR THE PERFECT PLACE TO TAKE A NAP.

KNOWING SHE IS SURROUNDED BY LOVE AND COMFORT,...

OLIVE FINALLY FALLS INTO A DEEP AND PEACEFUL SLEEP.

OLIVE

THE REAL OLIVE, WHOM THIS BOOK IS BASED UPON LIVES A HAPPY LIFE. HER PARENTS SPOIL HER, TREAT HER KINDLY, AND MAKE SURE SHE GETS TO DO ALL OF HER FAVORITE THINGS. THESE BOOKS ARE HER PARENTS' WAY OF KEEPING HER MEMORY ALIVE FOR EVERYONE TO SHARE. WE HOPE YOU ENJOY YOUR TIME WITH OUR OLIVE!

Made in the USA
Las Vegas, NV
08 April 2024

88410704R00017